This book belongs to

CHARLIE

UGLYDOLLS: TODAY'S THE DAY!

A CENTUM BOOK 978-1-913110-14-7

Published in Great Britain by Centum Books Ltd

This edition published 2019

1 3 5 7 9 10 8 6 4 2

Centum Books Ltd, 20 Devon Square, Newton Abbot, Devon, TQ12 2HR, UK

books@centumbooksltd.co.uk

CENTUM BOOKS Limited Reg. No. 07641486

A CIP catalogue record for this book is available
from the British Library.

Printed in China.

centum

UglyDolls

TODAY'S THE DAY!

Adapted by R.R. Busse

UGLYDOLLS

Meet the Ugly gang!

Moxy

Moxy is curious, confident and always wants to find out more.

Ox

Ox is the unofficial mayor of Uglyville. He keeps everyone safe.

Ugly Dog

Ugly Dog is always ready for a party, his pop-star swagger and MC skills give him super-confidence.

Wage

Wage is a cooking whizz who sometimes runs out of confidence – enter Moxy!

Babo

Babo is big, hungry and very handy.

Lucky Bat

Lucky Bat is wise, mysterious and always laid-back.

It's another bright, shiny morning in Uglyville. Moxy leaps out of her bed.

Today is THE day!

She runs over to her calendar and writes it down. She's *sure* that today's the day she will be chosen to go to the Big World and meet her human child!

**Moxy is so excited!
She looks at herself in a
mirror and starts singing:**

"Hello, gorgeous.
Let's check out how you look today:
Short and stubby,
Nubby teeth out on full display!
You're pinkish-red,
Got this thing on your head,
And WHOA—
Girl, you couldn't look better!"

Moxy is a reporter. Every day she writes *The Daily Ugly* and delivers her newspapers to all the UglyDolls in Uglyville with her friend Ugly Dog.

"Hey, Moxy!" he exclaims. "You're in a good mood!"

"That's because today I'm going to..."
Moxy says.

"Get chosen to go to the Big World and be with your child," Ugly Dog interrupts. "You say that every day."

"I know, but today..." Moxy belts out in excitement. "I might be right!"

**As Moxy and Ugly Dog make
their way through Uglyville,
Moxy continues her happy song:**

"Shake the sleep off—
And kick into the morning drill.
It's another awesome day
Here in Uglyville!
Grab your shoes,
Time to spread the good news!
Whoa! Things just couldn't be better!
Call it hope or faith, whatever!
I just know in my heart
It's the day I've awaited forever!"

Soon, they pass Wage's bakery. Wage is one of the best – if not *the* best – bakers in all of Uglyville. *"Mornin', Moxy!"* she sings through her window.

"Got something new you'll wanna try:
It's a brownie-cupcake-fudge-berry-ice-cream pie!
Just one bite – who needs kids, am I right?"

Moxy tries the crazy – delicious dessert while Wage tosses some to Babo, who is painting the outside of the bakery.

Babo is probably the strongest – and the sweetest – UglyDoll around. He's *always* hungry, and he can eat a whole pie in one bite!

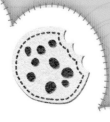

Next, Ugly Dog and Moxy see Ox and Lucky Bat. Ox is the mayor of Uglyville and knows that it's been a long time since an UglyDoll was chosen to go to the Big World. He doesn't want Moxy to be disappointed.

Ox hopes Lucky Bat will be able to talk some sense into her. Lucky Bat is Ox's most trusted adviser, and he's widely known as the wisest of all the UglyDolls.

The UglyDolls have a great time together, but Moxy can't stop thinking about meeting her child!

"When someone gets chosen, do you think they get picked up in a giant stretch dune buggy?" she asks.

Ox tries to distract Moxy.

"All this business about the so-called 'Big World' and children... it's just a fairy tale," he explains.
"Everyone says that, but what's the harm in believing?" Moxy asks.
"Never mind that," Ox starts to sing.

"I'll tell you what the day will bring—
First a shindig,
Then a bash, then more partying.
Top it all
With a rave, then a ball."

Suddenly, music fills the air and all the UglyDolls sing and dance together.

Ugly Dog jumps onstage and gets a chance to combine his three passions: rapping, sunglasses and backup lobsters.

Ox wants to remind Moxy she has everything she needs here, so he gives this song his all!

After his saxophone solo, he points out that Uglyville is the best place to be:

"You know it couldn't be better!"

Moxy gets into the groove after all her friends have joined in:

"And soon, you-know-what is comin'!"

"But until it arrives,
Might as well keep the party hummin'!"

the UglyDolls sing together.

After waiting and hoping all day, Moxy is a little sad. She wasn't picked for the Big World.

What if Ox is right? What if it really is all make-believe?

It can't be! If Moxy isn't going to get picked to meet her child... she'll pick her child herself!

Moxy gathers all her friends and declares,
"We're gonna make our dreams come true!"
With Lucky Bat, Wage, Ugly Dog and Babo,
she sets off to find the Big World. But what
they find instead is a mysterious tunnel.

Inside, the UglyDolls see a giant slide. The only way to see what's at the end of the slide is to *take it*!

At the bottom, they find themselves in front of a place called the Institute of Perfection. They don't know what 'perfection' is! They just know about being themselves.

INSTITUTE

Finding their kids might be harder than Moxy and her friends had thought. But anything is possible with good friends. And who knows, tomorrow might just be... *the day*!